For New End Primary School —J.D.

For Noah and Eva —L.M.

Henry Holt and Company, LLC, *Publishers since 1866*
175 Fifth Avenue, New York, New York 10010
mackids.com

Library of Congress Cataloging-in-Publication Data
Donaldson, Julia.
[What the ladybird heard]
What the ladybug heard / Julia Donaldson ; illustrated by Lydia Monks. — 1st American ed.
p.   cm.
Summary: Although much quieter than the farm animals that moo, cluck, or oink, a gentle ladybug is
instrumental in foiling a plan to steal the farm's prize-winning cow.
ISBN 978-0-8050-9028-4
[1. Stories in rhyme. 2. Ladybugs—Fiction. 3. Domestic animals—Fiction.
4. Animal sounds—Fiction. 5. Robbers and outlaws—Fiction.] I. Monks, Lydia, ill. II. Title.
PZ8.3.D7235Wg 2010   [E]—dc22   2009005266

First American Edition—2010
Printed in China by WKT Co., Ltd.

5 7 9 10 8 6

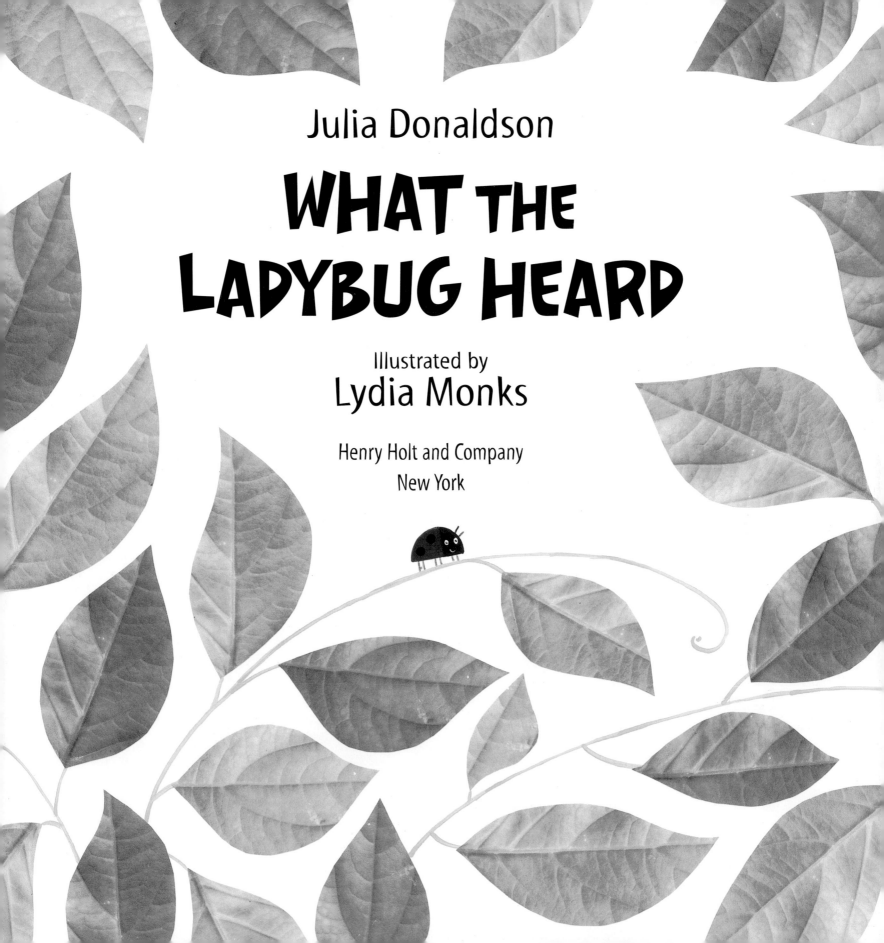

Julia Donaldson

WHAT THE LADYBUG HEARD

Illustrated by
Lydia Monks

Henry Holt and Company
New York

Once upon a farm there lived a fat red hen,
A duck in a pond and a goose in a pen,
A woolly sheep, a hairy hog,
A handsome horse and a dainty dog,
A fine prize cow, two cats that purred,

And a ladybug
who never said a word.

"NEIGH!" said the horse.

"OINK!" said the hog.

"BAA!" said the sheep.

"WOOF!" said the dog.

And one cat meowed while the other one purred . . .

...and the ladybug never said a word.

But the ladybug saw,
And the ladybug heard . . .

She saw two men in a big black van,
With a map and a key and a cunning plan.
And she heard them whisper, "This is how
We're going to steal the fine prize cow.

"Open the gate in the dead of night.
Pass the horse and then turn right.
Round the duck pond, past the hog
(Be careful not to wake the dog).
Left past the sheep, then straight ahead
And in through the door of the prize cow's shed!"

Then "Help!" was the ladybug's very first word,
And "Gather round" were the second and third.
And she told the animals, "This is how
Two thieves are planning to steal the cow:
They'll open the gate in the dead of night.
Pass the horse and then turn right.

Round the duck pond, past the hog
(Being careful not to wake the dog).
Left past the sheep, then straight ahead
And in through the door of the prize cow's shed!"

But the ladybug told them not to fear,
And she whispered her plan into every ear.

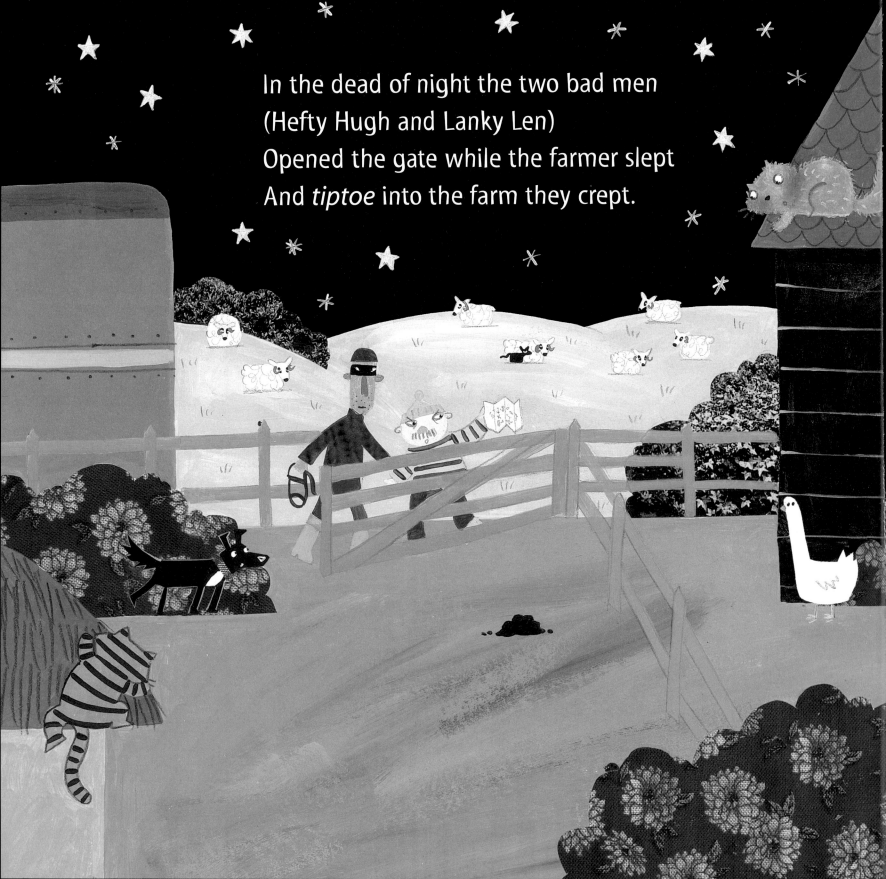

In the dead of night the two bad men
(Hefty Hugh and Lanky Len)
Opened the gate while the farmer slept
And *tiptoe* into the farm they crept.

Then the goose said, "NEIGH!" with all her might.
And Len said, "That's the horse—turn right."

NEIGH!

And the dainty dog began to QUACK.
"The duck!" said Hugh.
"We're right on track."

QUACK!

OINK! OINK!

"OINK!" said the cats.

"There goes the hog!
Be careful not to wake the dog."

"BAA BAA BAA!" said the fat red hen.
"The sheep! We're nearly there," said Len.

Then the duck on the pond said, "MOO MOO MOO!"
"Two more steps to go!" said Hugh.

And they both stepped into the duck pond—

SPLOSH!

And the farmer woke and said, "Golly gosh!"
And he called the cops, and they caught the men
(Hefty Hugh and Lanky Len).

Then the cow said, "MOO!"
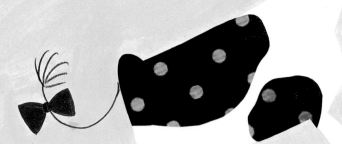

and the hen said, "CLUCK!"

"HISS!" said the goose

and "QUACK!" said the duck.